To Little
Trainspotters

This book belongs to

First published 1998 by Walker Books Ltd
87 Vauxhall Walk, London SE11 5HJ

This edition published 2000

2 4 6 8 10 9 7 5 3 1

© 1998 Charlotte Voake

This book has been typeset in Calligraphic.

Printed in Hong Kong

British Library Cataloguing in Publication Data
A catalogue record for this book is
available from the British Library.

ISBN 0-7445-7296-7

HERE COMES the TRAIN

CHARLOTTE VOAKE

WALKER BOOKS
AND SUBSIDIARIES
LONDON • BOSTON • SYDNEY

Every Saturday William, Chloe
and Dad go for a bike ride.
William sits on the back
of Dad's bike in his
little red seat.

They go across the golf course, through the woods, and out onto the footbridge.

The bridge is very high
and narrow, with railings
to stop people falling
over the edge.
And far below are
the railway tracks.
Dad lifts William out
of his seat and leans
his bike against the railings.
Sometimes Chloe has
a bit of trouble making
her bike stand up.

Then William and Chloe and Dad
look and listen for the trains.
It's very quiet and sometimes
they can see rabbits chasing
each other through
the bushes.

Sometimes workmen walk
along the railway with
shovels and spades
to mend the line.

Often other children and
people with dogs come
onto the bridge.

They all look at the signals.
When the lights change from
red to green ...

everyone on the bridge
hopes it means a train
is coming soon.

They all stare up
and down the line.

Then suddenly there it is,
a tiny speck in the distance!

William shouts,
"Here it comes...

HERE COMES
the TRAIN!"

Louder and louder,
nearer and nearer it comes!
Sparks shoot out
from its wheels!

All the children wave like mad.
The engine driver waves back;
he hoots his horn.
Beep-barp!

Beep - BARP

Everyone holds their
breath and ...

WHOOSH

under the bridge it goes!

Everyone's hair blows
in the wind.
The bridge rattles
and shakes.

Chloe SCREAMS because
she thinks it will fall down.
Everyone else screams
because they like screaming!

Afterwards,
when the train
has gone,
and it's quiet
again,

William,
Chloe and Dad
stand on the bridge
and wait ...

for the NEXT one!!!

At night, when William
goes to bed, if he's very quiet,
he can still hear the trains
in the distance.
And he whispers to himself,
"Here comes the train!
Here comes the train!
Here comes the train!"

before he falls fast asleep.

WALKER ❧ BOOKS

Here Comes the Train

CHARLOTTE VOAKE says that the idea for
Here Comes the Train is based on the real life experience
of going with her children (also Chloe and William) on
bikes to see the trains from a footbridge very like the
one in the book. "I had to do drawings at the bridge,"
she says, "and I got some funny looks and comments;
I think the men working on the tracks must have
thought I was a spy checking on them!"

Her many books include *Tom's Cat*; *Mrs Goose's Baby*
(shortlisted for the Best Books for Babies Award);
the Read and Wonder title *Caterpillar Caterpillar*
(shortlisted for the Kurt Maschler Award);
Mr Davies and the Baby and *Ginger*, which won
the Smarties Book Prize Gold Award (0–5 Category).
She lives in Surrey.

More Walker picture books for you to enjoy

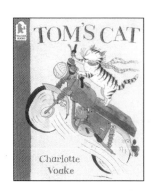

ISBN 0-7445-5272-9 (pb)

ISBN 0-7445-4791-1 (pb)

ISBN 0-7445-3636-7 (pb)

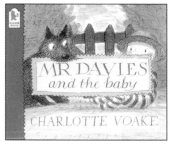

ISBN 0-7445-5237-0 (pb)